Boker Tov!
Good Morning!

To Sue, Elana and Ethan, who make
every morning bright – J.B.

To Kaitlin Sage and Grandpa Ron – R.B.

Text copyright © 2009 by Joe Black
Illustrations copyright © 2009 Lerner Publishing Group, Inc.

KAR-BEN Publishing
A division of Lerner Publishing Group, Inc.
241 First Avenue North
Minneapolis, MN 55401 U.S.A.
800-4KARBEN

Website address: www.karben.com

Library of Congress Cataloging-in-Publication Data

Black, Joe, 1959–
    Boker tov! : good morning! / by Rabbi Joe Black ; illustrated by Rick Brown.
      p.   cm.
    Summary: An illustrated version of a song about children waking up to a new
morning.
    ISBN 978–0–7613–3950–2 (lib. bdg. : alk. paper)
    1. Children's songs—United States–Texts. 2. Morning–Songs and music.
3. Jews—Songs and music. [1. Songs. 2. Morning—Songs and music.
3. Jews—Songs and music.] I. Brown, Richard E. (Richard Eric), 1946– ill.
II. Title.
PZ8.3.B5712Bo 2009
782.42—dc22 [E]   2008033481

Manufactured in the United States of America
1 2 3 4 5 6 7 – DP – 08 07 06 05 04 03

Boker Tov! Good Morning!

By Joe Black

Illustrated by
Rick Brown

KAR-BEN
PUBLISHING

Good morning, how do you do?

There's a new day
waiting for you.

Out of your jammies and into your clothes.

Boker tov!

Good morning, light shining in.
So much to do we can't wait to begin.

Gotta get going so
let's hit the road.

Boker tov!

Boker tov—it's a brand new day
Boker tov—good morning
—and we pray.

We thank God for the food we eat
For the earth beneath our feet...

For the morning sunshine bright,

That fills our hearts
with joy and light.
Boker tov!

Good morning, open your eyes.
Each new day brings
a brand new surprise.

Get it together
there's no time to doze.
Boker tov.

Good morning, let's sing our song.
Slept all night—
     now we're rested and strong.

Feeling so happy—
from our heads to our toes.
Boker tov!

Good morning, how do you do?
There's a new day waiting for you.

Out of your jammies
and into your clothes,

Boker tov!

Gotta get going so let's hit the road,

Boker tov.

Feeling so happy from
our heads to our toes.

Boker tov.

Boker Tov!

Joe Black is a congregational Rabbi, a singer, songwriter and guitarist whose infectious music for children and adults is celebrated and sung in Jewish communities throughout the United States, Canada and Israel. Rabbi Black's recordings have received accolades from sources as diverse as *The New York Times*, *Hadassah Magazine*, *Moment Magazine*, *Parent's Choice*, the *American Library Journal* and *Kids First: The Coalition for Quality Children's Video*. Joe is married to Sue Black and father to Elana and Ethan.